Shaking Hands with Michael Rooney

Tom Palmer

Illustrated by James Innerdale

Grassroots Football Fiction

D0228530

Published by
Grassroots Press
17a Bainbrigge Road
Headingley
Leeds
LS6 3AD

Made and printed in England by Ellset Creative Print, Yorkshire.

ISBN 1-901936-07-4

Tom Palmer's suspenseful tale taps into the daydreams that haunt the imaginations of soccer fans the world over.

Who hasn't fantasised about their gallant little club being drawn against one of the giants, and snatching victory to stun and confound the sneering pundits? Or scoring twice in stoppage time to clinch a title everybody assumed has slipped away.

Gripping and witty at the same time, Shaking Hands with Michael Rooney is quite simply the perfect soccer yarn.

Robert Swindells
Carnegie Medal winning author of *Stone Cold*

Shaking Hands with Michael Rooney will give you both the appetite to read more about football, and, through the fantastic Extra Time section, will show you how, through reading, you could become an expert on the game. You might want to be a top-flight footballer, but have you thought about becoming a top-flight football writer? Tom Palmer's tips are excellent and will keep you shooting on target.

Jim Sells
National Literacy Trust

Tom Palmer talks it like it's true and writes it like it's real. Here are characters painted sharp and clean. Here is a tale told with clarity and precision. If you've never read a novel before, then here's where you should start. If you've read loads and want one that jumps out at you, then try this one. Either way, just wait for the change of style that'll rocket you through the climax of this book. It works brilliantly. You'll feel like you're living and breathing it. This book kicks!'

Nick Toczek
Author of Kick It! Football Poems

for Iris – T.P.

for Dad, who took me to my first
football match - J.I.

Chapter One

Danny Harte's coach always said Danny was
going to be a great footballer.

And he must have been right, because
in his first year Danny had scored an average
of over two goals a game. And not just with his
legendary left foot. But with his right foot. His
head. And a couple off his knees.

His goal tally was up to thirty-four. Best in the Mordenshire League. With Jimmy Hassall of Athletico Armley close behind him, on twenty-seven.

Coach was well impressed.

'You're gonna be top scorer in the Mordenshire League this season,' he said.

'Am I?' Danny said.

'You are,' Coach said. 'And do you know what you get for being top?'

'No.' Danny had no idea.

'The golden boot!' Coach said. 'And not only that. You get to collect it at a big do at City Stadium in front of players from all over Mordenshire. And their families. In that posh banqueting suite they've got. There's always a first team player there to hand out the trophies. Look.' Coach pointed at a photograph on the wall. 'Here's a picture of Steven Lampard. The Premiership player. He played for us once. This is him winning the golden boot ten years ago. Who's your favourite player at the City Stadium, Danny? It might be him.'

'Rooney,' said Danny. 'Michael Rooney.'

Mordenshire League – Division One

Real Rothwell	15	12	3	0	+58	39
Athletico Armley	15	11	2	2	+45	35
Olympic Oxenhope	15	10	0	5	+13	30
Partizan Pudsey	15	7	1	7	+5	22
Bayern Beeston	15	7	0	8	-10	21
Inter Ilkley	15	4	5	6	-10	17
CSKA Clapham	15	4	4	7	-22	16
Sporting Seacroft	15	3	4	8	-17	13
Deportivo Denholme	15	2	6	7	-29	12
Hajduk Headingley	15	0	3	12	-33	3

Top Scorers

Danny Harte	Real Rothwell	34
Jimmy Hassall	Athletico Armley	27
Stu Manson	CSKA Clapham	16

Chapter Two

The next day, at school, Danny had to go to Mr Shearer's classroom to collect a box of books to bring back to his own class.

But he didn't want to do it.

And it wasn't *just* because Mr Shearer was the school's nastiest teacher. Danny had this thing, you see. He'd always had it. Ever since he could remember. Whenever he was in front of other people, and he had to carry something, his hands would shake. Walking in front of class 6B with a box of books would not be easy. Danny had been worrying about it all morning, trying to think of a way of getting out of it. But there was nothing he could do.

'Oh look. It's D-D-D-D Danny Harte,' Mr Shearer said as Danny knocked and entered the untidy classroom, bright sun streaming in through the large windows.

Nobody laughed. But Danny still felt stupid.

He picked up the box of books quickly and tried to carry it with his back to the class, so they wouldn't see him shaking. He jammed the box against his stomach and struggled out of the room.

Outside, Danny looked back through the small window in the door and saw Mr Shearer laughing. He felt like someone was tying a big knot in his stomach. So what if his hands shook a bit? he thought. They'd always shaken. Why did people always have to point it out, make fun of him?

But now he was out of Mr Shearer's class there was nothing else to worry about. Was there?

He walked off down the corridor. More relaxed now.

Half way back to his classroom he stopped in his tracks.

There *was* something else.

Danny felt sick.

If he had the shakes like this in front of class 6B, what was he going to be like in front of all those players from the Mordenshire leagues and their families? He wasn't going to be able to stand up and take the golden boot from... maybe from... Michael Rooney. His hands would shake so much he'd have to run out of the room and everyone would laugh at him. He'd never be able to show his face – or play football – again.

Danny realised that there was nothing else he could do: he was going to have to get out of collecting the golden boot. And to do that he'd have to stop scoring goals. He'd have to let Jimmy Hassall – who was a big mouth and had the biggest head in Mordenshire – finish top of the scoring charts.

There was no way he could go up in front of all those people.

Chapter Three

On Saturday morning, after Danny had missed half a dozen chances, making sure his shots only just went wide of the goal, or hit defenders instead of going into the net, Coach cornered him.

They'd lost 1-0. Their first defeat of the season. It meant that – if their big rivals, Athletico Armley had won today – Real Rothwell would be only one point ahead in the table.

'What was all that about today, Danny?' Coach said.

'What was all what about?' Danny said.

'You know what I'm talking about Danny.'

Danny was trying hard to think of things he'd heard real football players say on the TV after they hadn't played well.

'I didn't have my … er … touch today, Coach… And,' Danny went on. 'I didn't get the … the … rub of the green.'

Coach smiled. 'Well, so long as you're okay next week, Danny. We're playing Partizan Pudsey and we need you to get the … er… rub of the green back.'

He knows, Danny thought. He knows I'm missing goals on purpose. And maybe he knows why.

'I think I've picked up an injury as well,' Danny blurted out.

'I didn't notice anything,' Coach said.

'I did. It's my knee. I think it's my… my crucified ligament.'

'Do you now?' Coach said concealing a smile. 'Let's have a look.'

Coach studied Danny's knee.

'We'll have to keep an eye on you, won't we Danny?' Coach said.

Danny nodded, but he had the feeling that Coach knew what he was thinking. Knew that he was pretending to be injured. Knew that he wanted to miss the last games of the season on purpose. Knew everything.

Danny felt ashamed. He couldn't win either way.

If I do one thing it's scary, he thought. And if I do the other I'm letting everyone down.

Mordenshire League – Division One
Saturday 11th March

Athletico Armley	4	Deportivo Denholme	2
Bayern Beeston	9	Hajduk Headingley	0
Olympic Oxenhope	1	Sporting Seacroft	2
Partizan Pudsey	5	CSKA Clapham	2
Real Rothwell	0	Inter Ilkley	1

Real Rothwell	16	12	3	1	+57	39
Athletico Armley	16	12	2	2	+47	38
Olympic Oxenhope	16	10	0	6	+12	30
Partizan Pudsey	16	8	1	7	+8	25
Bayern Beeston	16	8	0	8	-1	24
Inter Ilkley	16	5	5	6	-9	20
Sporting Seacroft	16	4	4	8	-16	16
CSKA Clapham	16	4	4	8	-25	16
Deportivo Denholme	16	2	6	8	-31	12
Hajduk Headingley	16	0	3	13	-42	3

Top Scorers

Danny Harte	Real Rothwell	34
Jimmy Hassall	Athletico Armley	31
Stu Manson	CSKA Clapham	17

Chapter Four

'What am I gonna do?' said Danny.

'What's the problem?' Michael Rooney said.

'If I win the golden boot I can't collect it because my hands will shake… so I can't be top scorer in the league… so I have to stop scoring… and then we might not win the league… and they'll all blame me … so I'm going to have to pretend I'm injured.'

Whenever Danny had a problem he took it to Michael Rooney. All ever had to do was close his eyes and Michael Rooney would be there for him.

He might be an imaginary friend – but, if you were going to have an imaginary friend, Michael Rooney was the best one you could get.

Danny had asked Michael Rooney about all sorts of problems in the past. When those older boys who were bullying him and his friend Jatinder. That time when his dad shouted at his mum and didn't come home for a week. And that other time … when the dog died. But this new problem seemed like it was an even bigger problem than the rest put together.

'If it was me,' said Michael Rooney, 'I'd just score the goals because that's what I do. You want to be like me, don't you?'

'I do,' Danny said.

'Then just go ahead and play. And score all the goals you can.'

'But what happens when I get the ball and I can score, but I get that feeling that I'm scared again?'

'Do the right thing, Danny,' Michael Rooney said.

Chapter Five

Real Rothwell's next match was against Partizan Pudsey, the fourth best team in the league.

Danny's cousin, Harry Kelly, played for Partizan. He came over to Danny before kick off.

'Alright Danny?'

'Alright Harry.'

'How come you lost last week?' said Harry. 'I thought you had the league sewn up.'

Danny made some excuses. He said it had been an off day, that every team has to have a bad run during the season.

Harry patted Danny on the back, laughing. 'Well keep it up, will you? We could do with the three points today.'

The match kicked off.

It was a warm spring morning and there were lots of mums and dads on the touchline cheering both teams on.

The first time Danny got the ball in the box he passed it to Jatinder. But Jatinder was so surprised that Danny hadn't tried to score himself, he wasn't ready for the ball and kicked it into some trees.

The second time Danny got the ball – in front of an open goal – he shot, aiming for the bar, and, just like he'd wanted, it bounced off the top and went behind for a goal kick.

'Bad luck, Danny,' his cousin said, coming over to him and patting him on the back again.

The third time Danny got the ball, he decided not to shoot, but to run with the ball and wait until he was tackled. But the tackle came in like a tonne of bricks, sending Danny flying. And he heard the ref's whistle.

'Penalty!'

Danny stood up quickly and walked away from the penalty area.

'Come on Danny,' Jatinder said. 'Penalty.'

Danny always took the penalties.

'You take it,' Danny said to Jatinder. 'My leg doesn't feel right. I think I've... I've... picked up a knock.'

Jatinder looked at Coach standing on the touchline.

'No Jatinder,' Coach said. 'Danny's taking it.'

Danny felt cold. He walked up to the penalty spot. It was as if he was on the pitch by himself. Just him, the ball and the gaping goal.

What was he going to do?

It was 0-0. The team needed a goal. If they won the game one-nil they'd still be able to win the league. If they drew or lost – and other results didn't go their way – it could be a disaster.

Danny looked around at all his team mates.

'Go on Danny!' they were shouting, big smiles on their faces. They knew that Danny Harte never missed a penalty.

Danny worked out a plan.

He decided that if he fired the ball hard against the post it would come back into play and one of the others could score the goal. It was simple.

He stepped up to the penalty spot and struck the ball.

It seemed to take an age to hit the post. And when it came back at *him* he ducked.

He knew it was in the rules: if a penalty taker hits the post he's not allowed to touch it until someone else touches it.

The ball flew back towards a scrum of players and a Partizan Pudsey defender hoofed it out for a throw in.

Coach shouted across the pitch. 'Danny Harte! You're coming off.'

'But…' Danny said.

'Off!' Coach said.

Danny decided not to argue with Coach. He knew that if he'd really wanted to score he could have. He knew he deserved this punishment.

So – for the first time in his life – Danny Harte was substituted.

And with Danny off the pitch it all went wrong. Real Rothwell lost 2-0.

Mordenshire League – Division One
Saturday 18th March

Athletico Armley	5	Olympic Oxenhope	2
CSKA Clapham	4	Inter Ilkley	0
Deportivo Denholme	3	Bayern Beeston	3
Real Rothwell	0	Partizan Pudsey	2
Sporting Seacroft	6	Hajduk Headingley	1

Athletico Armley	17	13	2	2	+49	41
Real Rothwell	17	12	3	2	+55	39
Olympic Oxenhope	17	10	0	7	+11	30
Partizan Pudsey	17	9	1	7	+10	28
Bayern Beeston	17	8	1	8	-1	25
Inter Ilkley	17	5	5	7	-13	20
Sporting Seacroft	17	5	4	8	-11	19
CSKA Clapham	17	5	4	8	-21	19
Deportivo Denholme	17	2	7	8	-31	13
Hajduk Headingley	17	0	3	14	-47	3

Top Scorers

Danny Harte	Real Rothwell	34
Jimmy Hassall	Athletico Armley	34
Stu Manson	CSKA Clapham	19

Chapter Six

In the changing rooms after the game, everyone was nearly dressed and ready to go. A couple of the lads were reading magazines as they waited for others to finish. One was reading *Match*. Another *Shoot!* The two central defenders – Luke and Dom – were whispering to each other and looking over at Danny.

Danny sat alone, his head down, not looking at anyone. Until he was sure he was the last one there.

At last, thinking everyone was gone, he made his way out to go home.

But Jatinder was waiting outside.

'What's up, Danny?'

'Nothing.'

'Everyone's saying stuff,' Jatinder said.

'What stuff? Who?' Danny said.

'Luke and Dom. They're saying you missed the penalty on purpose.'

Danny felt the knot tighten in his stomach again. He didn't dare look his friend in the face.

Jatinder went on. 'They're saying your cousin paid you off – paid you to miss the penalty. It's not true, is it?'

Danny just looked at the ground.

He felt like the world was collapsing around him as Jatinder walked off across the playing fields.

Chapter Seven

It was the last day of the season.

Real Rothwell were away to Athletico Armley. First versus second. Athletico were two points clear. To win the league, Real had to beat Athletico. A draw wouldn't be enough.

Jimmy Hassall was playing up front for Athletico. He had caught up with Danny now. They had thirty-four goals each. And Jimmy was scoring at least two goals a game.

He was bound to score today. And, seeing as Danny wasn't even playing, Jimmy Hassall would take the golden boot. Easy.

In a way, Danny had got just what he wanted.

But he didn't feel very good about it.

Sitting at home – having pretended to his mum there was no game, too scared to turn up and face his team mates – he closed his eyes and imagined Michael Rooney was next to him again.

'What shall I do?'

'Play!' Michael Rooney said.

'But I'm not in the team,' said Danny.

'Then go and watch,' said Rooney. 'They're your team. They need you.'

'But they all hate me.'

'Well if they do, they're wrong,' Michael Rooney said.

'They're not wrong. They're right! I did miss the penalty on purpose. If it wasn't for me we'd have won the league by now.'

'Go and cheer them on,' Michael Rooney said.

'Why?'

'It's better than sitting here feeling sorry for yourself.'

Chapter Eight

The players were already warming up when Danny got to the pitch. He saw Coach and tried to hide behind a tree, but Coach caught up with him.

'Hello Danny.'

'Hello,' Danny mumbled.

'I thought you weren't coming,' Coach said.

'I didn't think you'd want me.'

'Don't be silly, Danny. We always want you here. You're our top scorer, aren't you?' Coach was smiling. 'Listen,' he went on. 'I can't put you in the team because I've already given the names to the referee. But you can be sub if you like.'

'Do the others want me?' Danny said.

Coach knelt down next to him and sighed. 'Danny Harte! All that stuff about your cousin bribing you is rubbish. You know it. I know it. And the rest of the team know it. I am not sure what the matter is with you at the moment, but we all know you're a nice lad and that you'd never do anything like that. Now go and sit on the bench.'

Coach pointed at two upturned plastic buckets.

By half time Athletico Armley were winning 2-1. Jimmy Hassall had scored both which meant he was two goals ahead of

Danny in the goal scoring chart. If it stayed like this Athletico Armley would come top of the league.

Real Rothwell needed to turn it round.

Danny stayed away from the other players at half time, even though Coach had told him everything was okay. Then Danny saw Luke and Dom coming over.

He felt the knot in his stomach tighten so much it hurt.

'Alright Danny?' Luke said.

'Alright.'

'You playing?' Dom said.

'What?'

'You playing, Danny? We need you.'

Danny felt the knot in his stomach loosen.

'Yeah,' he said. 'I'm playing.' And every time I get the ball, he thought, I'm gonna score.

Chapter Nine

Welcome to the second half of this thrilling championship decider... and the big news is that, Real Rothwell are bringing on their top scorer, Danny Harte. Harte's been unavailable, probably injured, but it looks like they're going to risk him. There's everything to play for...

Real kick off. There's a good thirty people watching today. This is such a crucial game. Everything to play for...

… the ball's gone out for a corner… the centre back sends it high into the penalty box … and there's young Harte. His first touch. Danny Harte! He shoots. It's a goal! Two-all. There's hope for Rothwell. All they need is one more goal and they're champions…

... a long ball up field... Jatinder Singh is onto it. He takes it past one player, then the next. And Harte's in space! Singh lays in the perfect ball. Harte shoots. OHHHHH! It's hit the post. But it's back with Harte. On the rebound. He shoots again. It's three-two. Three-two to Real Rothwell. And their star striker – Danny Harte – has brought them back from the dead. Their season looked to be in tatters, but this young man has turned things round. Two goals in ten minutes. And added to that... he's now level with Jimmy Hassall for the golden boot...

45

… a rare attack up the other end… Jimmy Hassall's one-on-one with the keeper. And it's a goal. It's all gone quiet. It's three-three. And not only are Rothwell's championship hopes in ruins, but Jimmy Hassall heads the scoring charts again. It looks like it's not going to be such a great day for young Danny Harte, after all. What do you think, Trevor?

Well, Danny's got a heart of gold, but…

…sorry to interrupt you there Trevor, but here's Harte again – the very player you were speaking about – he's taken on half the Armley team. He's gone past them all. The keeper's come out. But what's Harte doing? He's side footed it. He was about to shoot. It's like he didn't want to score at all! But – just a minute – there's Singh running onto Harte's pass. Jatinder Singh. From nowhere! And it's 4-3. What a shot! What a game!

*4-3 to Real Rothwell and… I don't believe it …
the referee has blown his whistle. Real 4
Athletico 3. Rothwell are champions. And the
only consolation for Athletico is that their star
striker, Jimmy Hassall, is leading scorer and
it'll be him who collects the golden boot on
Sunday at the special reception at the City
Stadium. Trevor…'*

Mordenshire League – Division One
Saturday 25th March

Athletico Armley	3	Real Rothwell	4
Bayern Beeston	4	Inter Ilkley	2
Deportivo Denholme	4	Hajduk Headingley	5
Olympic Oxenhope	4	Partizan Pudsey	6
Sporting Seacroft	2	CSKA Clapham	5

Real Rothwell	18	13	3	2	+56	42
Athletico Armley	18	13	2	3	+48	41
Partizan Pudsey	18	10	1	7	+12	31
Olympic Oxenhope	18	10	0	8	+9	30
Bayern Beeston	18	9	1	8	+1	28
Inter Ilkley	18	5	5	8	-15	20
CSKA Clapham	18	6	4	8	-18	22
Sporting Seacroft	18	5	4	9	-14	19
Deportivo Denholme	18	2	7	9	-32	13
Hajduk Headingley	18	1	3	14	-46	6

Top Scorers

Jimmy Hassall	Athletico Armley	37
Danny Harte	Real Rothwell	36
Stu Manson	CSKA Clapham	20

Chapter Ten

At the City Stadium the following Sunday, Danny felt a bit funny watching Jimmy Hassall collect the golden boot. And from the real Michael Rooney too.

Now he was at the ceremony – and he'd gone up with the rest of the team to collect the league winner's trophy – he didn't see what he had been so worried about. He could have managed. Shakes or no shakes. He didn't really care what people thought about him.

Michael Rooney bent down and say a few words to Jimmy Hassall.

That should have been me, Danny thought. He could have been saying those things to me.

He felt sick. He was just about to go to the toilet, so he could think, when he heard his name being called out.

'Danny Harte...'

What was all this about? He looked up to see the man with the microphone – talking about *him*.

'A special prize ... the first time it's been awarded, in fact... voted for by all the coaches from all the teams in the Mordenshire League. So it's a very special award. Player of the season. Real Rothwell FC's Danny Harte!'

Danny looked over at Coach, who was smiling.

'I forgot to tell you about this prize, Danny. Didn't I?'

And Danny was walking towards the stage.

He could feel his hands shaking and his knees trembling and his head wobbling and his heart pumping, and he had a great big smile across his face because he didn't care. He could shake all he liked and everyone could see him shake. So what? he thought. So what?

And, when he looked up, Michael Rooney had the player of the season trophy in one hand and was holding his other hand out to shake hands with Danny.

And Danny wondered, although he couldn't be sure, whether Michael Rooney's hand wasn't shaking a bit too.

Extra Time

How to become a world class
football reader and writer

Interview with football writer Tom Palmer

Tom Palmer has written four books. Two of them about football. We asked him a few questions.

Do you like football or books best?
Both.

But if you could only have football or books – or else you'd be shot – what would you choose?
I'd rather be shot.

How did you become a football writer?
I love football. I got into writing about it because I started reading about it. So it was being a football reader that made me a football writer.

Okay. So, how did you become a football reader?
At first, I hated reading. I was doing really badly at school. My mum gave up trying to get me to read 'proper books'. They were boring. Instead, she got me loads of stuff to read

about football. Newspapers. Magazines. Books about how to play. Encyclopaedias. Stories. And I liked them because I was interested in them. That's how.

So you hated reading?
Yes. To be honest I couldn't read more that a page at a time. I couldn't concentrate. My mum started me with short things – like football reports in the newspaper and magazine articles. And she used to take me to matches because nobody else would – even though she hated football.

Did she really hate football?
I don't know. Leeds was a frightening place to go then. Lots of fighting in the stadium. She was scared of it – a bit, I think. But she still took me.

How many times did she take you?
Fifty or more. And she used to buy the match day programme every time we went. Part of her trying to get me to enjoy reading.

And do you enjoy reading?
I do now. I love it. It changed my life. If I hadn't got into reading I'd never have been sent all over Europe just to watch football and write about it.

What's the best football stadium you've been to?
Real Madrid. My first job as a professional writer was to go to Madrid and write about Leeds playing there. The stadium was the best I'd ever seen. I never dreamed I'd be paid to go and watch Leeds, get into the stadium ten feet from Alan Smith and Rio Ferdinand and write about it.

So, that was your first job? How did you get a book published?
I sent the thing I wrote about Madrid to a publisher and they asked me to write a book about a whole season supporting Leeds. That's the best way of getting published. You write something short and send it to a publisher and say, This is what I can do.

What other jobs can you do if you write about football?

You could be a football commentator – you need to be able to put words together and to have read a lot about football in newspapers. Also, you can get a job writing the story behind a football computer game. Or be sent to the World Cup to watch all the games and write about them. There's lots you can do.

Is it hard being a Leeds Fan?

No.

Are you sure?

Yes. It's great being a Leeds fan.

But Leeds are not very good anymore, are they?

We're not in European semis every year, but we're still pretty good. Anyway, it doesn't matter if your football team is good: it's that it's your football team. And, we'll be back. Back in the Premiership and back in the Champions' League.

Sure you will. Next question: if you didn't support Leeds who would you support?
No one.

No really, if you had to support Man U or Chelsea – or you'd get shot again – who would you support?
You'd better get your gun.

Do you play football?
I used to. But I did my knee in.

What position?
Striker.

Were you good?
No. I was alright with my mates. I could score ten goals in a game. But when I got into proper organised games – with tactics and all that – I was rubbish.

Which football book do you wish you'd written?
Cool by Michael Morpurgo. I think it's the perfect football story.

That's a story. What about non-fiction?
A book called *Fever Pitch*. It was the first really good book about what it's like to be a normal football fan.

Where do you get books you want to read?
In the library and at bookshops. I try to borrow as many books as I can – because books are expensive. But if I really want one, and I can afford it, I buy it.

What was the last book you bought?
A story about a goalkeeper who is trained to be the best keeper in the world – by a ghost. It's called *Keeper* and it's by Mal Peet. It's amazing.

What's your favourite football magazine?
It used to be *Shoot* or *Match*. But now it's *FourFourTwo*.

Who's the most famous footballer you've met?
Peter Schmiechel

What did you say to him?
Nothing. I was too nervous.

Tom Palmer's Top Ten Football Stories

1   *Cool* by Michael Morpurgo
2   *Keeper* by Mal Peet
3   *Match of Death* by James Riordan
4   *The Big Match* by Rob Childs
5   *Sudden Death* by Neil Arksey
6   *The Transfer* by Terrence Blacker
7   *Dream On* by Bali Rai
8   *Bend It Like Beckham* by Narinder Dhami
9   *Bad Boyz: Barmy Army* by Alan Durrant
10   *War Game* by Michael Foreman

Finding football stories (also called novels and fiction) in **libraries** *is easy. They will be in the junior fiction and teenage fiction sections. The books will be in A to Z order by the author's last name.*

If you need help in finding the section ask the librarian. They will know where all the best football stories are if you can't find any under A to Z. If you want a specific book the librarian can look it up on the computer to check if they have it on the shelves.

Joining the library is free. And easy. Just ask. And someone will be pleased help you.

Bookshops *are the same as libraries for football fiction. There is normally a children's section. If you have problems, ask a bookseller.*

Five tips on becoming a football writer

1. Read anything you can about football – from the back page of a newspaper to books.

2. Buy a notebook. Stick football pictures on the cover. Write down anything you are interested in to do with football. A match you've seen on TV. Something funny you've heard on Five Live. Something out of a newspaper or a book.

3. Write something every day. Even if it's just one line. Keep a diary of football in your life. Writing is like training for football. The more you practice the better you get.

4. Write like you speak. You don't have to use big words. If this is hard, try recording your voice talking about football and write it down. That's your voice. No one can speak or write exactly like you do.

5. Once you've written a few things, show someone you trust what you've done. Ask them what they like about it and what they think could be made better.

…and a final bit of advice.

You *can* write. *Everyone* can write. Don't let anyone tell you otherwise.

Tom Palmer's Top Ten Football Non Fiction Books

1   *Fever Pitch* by Nick Hornby
2   *Kick It, Poems* by Nick Toczek
3   *Foul Football* by Michael Coleman
4   *Sky Sports Football Yearbook*
5   *Great Big Quiz Book* by Michael Coleman
6   *Big Match Manager* by Tom Sheldon
7   *A Season with Verona* by Tim Parks
8   *Football Against the Enemy* by Simon Kuper
9   *Michael Owen's Soccer Skills*
10   *My Side* by David Beckham

*Football non-fiction can be found in several places in **libraries**. Try junior non-fiction for a start; then, in the adult books section, under Sport and Biography.*

If you want a specific book the librarian can look it up on the computer to check if they have it on the shelves.

***Bookshops** are the same as libraries for football non-fiction, as with fiction. If you have problems ask a bookseller.*

Five tips on becoming a football reader

1. Don't tell yourself that you hate reading or that you're not a Reader. You're reading this, so it can't be true!

2. Make a list of everything you read about football in one day. Did you read Teletext? The Internet? The back of the paper? See how much you read. It doesn't have to be books. Reading is reading anything. Maybe the list you make will show you that you are a big reader already.

3. Read what you want to. Find books and magazines and newspapers that you'll enjoy.

4. The best way to find what books you like and don't like is to go to the library – where all books are free. It's easy to join and libraries aren't places where only clever people go and you have to be quiet. Libraries are for you. For everyone. The staff who work in them can help you find what you want.

5. If you're reading a book and you think it's boring, you don't have to finish it, unless it's one you need to finish for school. Try another 10 pages and if it's still boring, give up and start a new book. That includes this book. I don't finish half the books I read. I don't read to be bored. I read to enjoy myself.

Great football reading on the Internet and on Teletext

The Internet has some great websites about football. These are Tom Palmer's favourite five:

www.bbc.co.uk/football
www.thefa.com
www.literacytrust.org.uk/football
www.footballguardian.co.uk
www.lufc.co.uk
(but, if you don't support Leeds, there'll be a club website for you)

Teletext is available on most TV channels. In total there are probably 1000s of pages available – most of them updated quicker than newspapers and the internet. It's a good place to keep up with scores.

But you probably already knew that.

You need to key in a three digit number to find the right page. The BBC football page is 302. There's an index on all Teletext channels to help you find your way to football.

Tom Palmer's top ten football newspaper pages

There are lots of newspapers, each printing from 3 to 25 pages about football each day. There might be newspapers lying about your house, but, if not, you can read newspapers for free in most libraries. Big libraries can have more than 10 newspapers – small ones up to five. All free. You can just go in, pull up a chair and read all day if you like.

The Daily Express
The Guardian
The Independent
The Daily Mail
Metro
The Daily Mirror
The Star
The Sun
The Telegraph
The Times

Always check out your local newspapers too. If you support the local club this is usually the best place to find out what's really happening at your club.

Tom Palmer's Top Eight Football Magazines

1   *FourFourTwo*
2   *Match*
3   *When Saturday Comes*
4   *Shoot*
5   *World Soccer*

You might not fancy the next three magazines – if you don't support Leeds! But your club should have its own versions.

6   *Leeds! Leeds! Leeds!*
7   *Leeds Matchday Programme*
8   *Square Ball – Leeds United fanzine*

Some libraries have copies of Match *and* Shoot *that you can read for free. Otherwise the best places for magazines are newsagents and WHSmiths.*
You can get programmes and fanzines, outside the ground before a game.

Acknowledgements:

Shaking Hands with Michael Rooney was originally commissioned by Leeds Libraries – to be read for performance. The author owes Leeds Libraries a lot. They commissioned his first piece of professional writing in 2002. They commissioned this story. But, most importantly, they provided him with unlimited numbers of books for free when he decided he liked reading, age seventeen.

Thank you to Rebecca and Iris Palmer. For everything.

Thanks also to Britta Heyworth, James Innerdale, James Nash, Jim Sells, Nick Toczek, Nikki Woodman, Robert and Brenda Swindells, Bernard Murphy and Gareth, Rory and Cal.

About the author

Tom hated reading until he was 17. It was reading about football that helped make him love reading. Now he is a football writer. He has written fiction and non-fiction as well as for magazines and newspapers, including the *Observer.* Tom works for the National Literacy Trust and The Football Foundation on the Premier League Reading Stars scheme. He has also worked for the BBC, Booktrust, The Reading Agency, the British Council Literature Department. He runs his popular Football Reading Game in libraries and schools around the country. He lives in Yorkshire with his wife and daughter.

About the illustrator

James Innerdale is a freelance artist and illustrator. His fresh witty and engaging style has been used successfully on a variety of subjects. Recent work includes drawings for a series of short childrens stories about life in the Yorkshire Dales and a range of illustrated maps and interpretation panels. In addition a regular cartoon strip for a national building conservation periodical utilises his architectural background. James now lives in the Yorkshire Dales but remains an ardent Brighton fan and is delighted to be able to illustrate his love of football.